ALL about WILD ANIMALS

PENGUINS

Please visit our website, www.garethstevens.com. For a free color catalog of all our high-quality books, call toll free 1-800-542-2595 or fax 1-877-542-2596.

Library of Congress Cataloging-in-Publication Data

All about penguins.
Penguins.
p. cm. – (All about wild animals)
Previously published in Great Britain as: All about penguins. 2002.
ISBN-10: 0-8368-4186-7 ISBN-13: 978-0-8368-4186-2 (lib. bdg.)
1. Penguins–Juvenile literature. I. Title. II. Series.
QL696.S473A424 2004
598.47–dc22 2004040810

This edition first published in 2005 by
Gareth Stevens Publishing
111 East 14th Street, Suite 349
New York, NY 10003

Editorial and design: Tucker Slingsby Ltd., London
Gareth Stevens series editor: Catherine Gardner
Gareth Stevens art direction: Tammy West

Picture Credits
NHPA – B and C Alexander: Front cover, title page, 14, 24–25, 28; G. I Bernard: 6; Rich Kirchner: 7; Kevin Schafer: 9, 17; Brian Hawkes: 13; Daniel Heuclin: 18; A.N.T. Photo Library: 19; Gerard Lacz: 21; Dave Watts: 22; Bill Coster: 23; John Shaw: 23, 26; Jonathan and Angela Scott: 27.
Oxford Scientific Films – Tui De Roy: 10; Doug Allan: 11, 16, 20–21; Howard Hall: 12–13; Daniel Cox: 13, 15; Robin Bush: 19; Bruce Herod: 29.

Printed in the United States of America

2 3 4 5 6 7 8 9 08 07

ALL about WILD ANIMALS

PENGUINS

Gareth Stevens
PUBLISHING

Penguin Facts

Animal Group: bird

Color: black and white body with yellow, orange, or red bill or other markings in some types.

Size: up to 4 feet (1.2 meters) tall

Weight: From 45 to 90 pounds (20 to 40 kilograms)

Speed: swims as fast as 9 miles (14 kilometers) per hour but walks less than 2 miles (3.2 km) per hour

Eats: fish, squid, and shellfish

Drinks: seawater

Lives: up to 25 years

Words that appear in the glossary are printed in **boldface** type the first time they occur in the text.

CONTENTS

A Closer Look

Penguins are birds. Unlike most kinds of birds, penguins cannot fly. Instead, penguins are made for swimming. A penguin's body is smooth and **streamlined**, and its wings are shaped like paddles. The penguin flaps its wings as if it were flying through the water and uses its webbed feet and stubby tail to steer. On land, most kinds of penguins **waddle**, but some hop or slide.

DID YOU KNOW?

- Penguins have short, stiff feathers with tufts of **down** at the base of each feather. The feathers overlap, so they trap lots of air. The layers of air and feathers keep penguins warm and dry in their cold home.

- The feathers of penguins are packed together more closely than the feathers of most other kinds of birds. A penguin has as many as fifteen feathers in a space about the size of a child's fingertip.

- When a penguin is hot, it **ruffles** its feathers and holds its wings out from its sides to cool down.

My oily feathers are waterproof.
My flipper-shaped wings are great for swimming.
I have a smooth shape so I can glide easily in the water.
Under my skin is a thick layer of fat, or blubber, that keeps me warm.
My tail and feet help me turn when I swim.
On land, I use my feet to stand and walk. I'm not very fast on the ice.

Penguins live on the land and in the sea. They can see well when they are underwater, but they do not have sharp vision on land. Penguins have good hearing, and they keep in touch with each other by using a series of different calls.

A penguin also sends messages to other penguins by using the position of its head, beak, and body.

Eye, Eye

Special clear eyelids protect the penguin's eyes. The eyelids let the penguin see underwater but keep the ice-cold, salty water from hurting the bird's eyes.

Did You Know?

- A penguin uses its bill to catch its food. The inside of the penguin's mouth is covered with spines that point backward. The spines help the penguin grip and swallow wiggly fish.

- A bill is a handy tool for **preening**. A penguin uses its bill to remove dirt and to spread oil from its body over its feathers to keep them waterproof.

- A penguin gets rid of salt from its body through special parts of its bill. As a result, a penguin can drink seawater without becoming ill.

Home, Sweet Home

All penguins live only in the southern half of the world, but different kinds of penguins live in different **habitats**. Some kinds stay in the icy water around Antarctica. Others settle near the coasts of New Zealand or South America or in the warmer water near South Africa and the Galapagos Islands. Penguins spend most of their time at sea. Many only go ashore to **molt** and to lay their eggs.

Super Sliders

An emperor penguin usually slides or waddles over the ice to reach its **breeding** ground. If it needs to move even faster, it toboggans down icy slopes on its belly. It's a quick – and fun – way to move!

Where in the World?

Emperor penguins live on Antarctica's **pack ice** and in the water around this big continent, which is almost twice the size of Australia. Antarctica is the coldest place on Earth, and ice covers the land. Emperor penguins have thick blubber and wind-blocking feathers to help them stay warm.

Did You Know?

- In Antarctica, the Sun never sets in summer, but in winter, it stays dark twenty-four hours a day.
- The lowest temperature on Earth was -129° Fahrenheit (-89° Celsius). It was recorded in Antarctica.
- Antarctica is swept by winds of up to 198 miles (320 kilometers) per hour.
- It's so cold in Antarctica that a metal bar would shatter like glass if it were dropped on the ground.

Warm Burrows

Magellanic penguins live in cold coastal waters around Chile and Argentina. They make their nests in deep **burrows**, where their baby chicks stay until they grow adult feathers.

Neighbors

A huge sheet of ice almost completely covers Antarctica. In this icy place, very little survives on land, except for a few plants and tiny insects. The seas around Antarctica swarm with life. Very small animals and plants, such as krill and plankton, drift through the water or float at the surface. They are eaten by bigger creatures, such as fish, squids, seals, seabirds, and even the big whales that live in the water around Antarctica.

Hungry Hunter

The sperm whale is the largest of the whales with teeth. It grows up to 65 feet (20 meters) long and weighs about as much as ten elephants. Sperm whales eat a lot. Some of their favorite foods are squids and fish. One sperm whale had about twenty-eight thousand small squids in its stomach at one time!

Noisy Nose!

A male elephant seal, known as a bull, has a big nose that looks like a short trunk. He makes loud sounds to attract **mates** and warn other males to stay away. His big nose makes his calls louder so they can be heard far away.

Wide Wings

Wandering albatrosses swoop and glide over the seas around Antarctica as they search for fish to eat. With wings that stretch nearly 10 feet (3 m) from tip to tip, wandering albatrosses have longer wingspans than any other living birds. They can fly 500 miles (800 km) in a day and stay over water for months.

The Family

Emperor penguins often live and swim together, but they usually hunt alone. They breed on the Antarctic pack ice in big groups called rookeries. Male and female emperor penguins usually pair for life. At breeding time, they call and search for each other on the pack ice. Their calls can be heard from .6 mile (1 km) away.

A female emperor penguin lays one egg between May and July, which is winter in Antarctica. Emperor penguins do not build nests. Instead, a penguin carries its egg on top of its feet, covering the egg with its lower body. The female and male share the job at first. Then the female returns to the sea to feed, and the male looks after the egg all alone. He keeps the egg covered with a special flap of skin on his belly.

Top Dad

The male emperor penguin is a good father. He warms an egg on his feet for as long as two months. While he cares for the egg, he cannot eat, so he may lose half his body weight! To keep his own body warm as he waits, he huddles close to the other male penguins.

Keeping Warm

A young penguin chick has fluffy gray feathers. It stays warm and snug, resting on its mother's feet and hiding beneath her feathers. Older chicks and adults huddle in groups, taking turns on the colder outside edge.

Baby File

Birth

The father **incubates** the egg for about sixty days. Just before the egg hatches, the mother usually carries the egg. When the chick hatches, it stays warm and safe on its mother's feet.

Six Weeks

The chick grows quickly as it eats food **regurgitated** by its parents. When it is six or seven weeks old, it snuggles up with the other chicks while its parents hunt.

Four to Six Months

Young penguins lose their downy feathers and grow adult ones. As summer returns to Antarctica, the young penguins go to sea to hunt by themselves.

Life on the Ground

Most birds spend little time on the ground and fly away if they spot enemies. Some birds, like penguins, cannot fly. **Flightless** birds developed on islands and in remote areas where they had few enemies. Some flightless birds, such as the ostrich, are large and fast. They can run away from **predators**. The kiwi and other small flightless birds avoid enemies by hiding among tall plants and shrubs.

Big Kickers

Cassowaries live in rain forests in Australia. They are large birds that stand almost as tall as adult humans. Cassowaries eat roots and berries and are peaceful birds, except if predators attack. When it faces an enemy, a cassowary lashes out with its large, spiked feet. It strikes with slashing blows that are deadly enough to kill a person.

DID YOU KNOW?

The dodo was a flightless bird about the size of a turkey. It lived on islands in the Indian Ocean. As people moved to settle on these islands, they began to hunt the dodo for food. People who settled on the islands also brought pets and other animals that were new to the habitat. Dodoes were easy **prey** for the new predators. The last dodoes on Earth died out more than two hundred years ago.

Shy Birds

Many birds in New Zealand, such as kiwis, cannot fly. Until people arrived about one thousand years ago, no big predators lived there. Birds did not need to fly to escape from their enemies. The shy kiwi hides by day and hunts at night. It sniffs out insects and pecks at them with its long bill.

Rare Parrot

The New Zealand kakapo, also called an owl parrot, is one of the rarest birds in the world. Kakapos cannot fly, but they can run fast on the ground and glide in the air. The kakapo climbs a tree using its bill and its claws, and then it glides down about 330 feet (100 m).

Favorite Foods

Penguins are predators. They hunt fish, shrimps, and squids. A penguin grabs its prey with its sharp-tipped bill and swallows food without chewing. In summer, penguins must gobble up as much food as possible to build up a thick layer of blubber. Blubber helps keep them warm and healthy through the winter.

Daring Diver

Unlike flying birds, penguins do not have light, air-filled bones. They have solid, heavy bones that make it easier for penguins to dive deep into the icy ocean and stay underwater for many minutes.

Did You Know?

- Emperor penguins can dive to depths of 850 feet (260 m), and they stay underwater for as long as twenty minutes – longer than any other bird.
- Penguins may travel up to 620 miles (1,000 km) in search of food.

Fishing off the Coast

Humboldt penguins live along the coast of Peru and Chile. They make nests by burrowing into large piles of seabird droppings that form in caves and along cliffs. From their coastal homes, Humboldt penguins snack on fish. To hunt for a meal, they dive into the water and grab tasty fish with their pointed bills.

Hunter or Hunted?

Squids are predators, too. They glide silently through the water, catching their prey in their long tentacles. If danger threatens, a squid speeds away by shooting out a jet of water. Squids may be quick, but they are no match for a powerful penguin. It takes a penguin just one big gulp to swallow a small squid!

Danger!

An adult emperor penguin has few enemies when it rests on Antarctica's ice. The main threats are cold weather and starvation. Penguin chicks and eggs are fast food for large seabirds that often swoop down to the pack ice for meals. In the sea, penguins must watch for many more predators. Seals, sea lions, sharks, and killer whales all like penguins for dinner.

Cool Killers

Killer whales, or orcas, are deadly predators. They can tip over an **ice floe** and gobble up the penguins resting on top.

Did You Know?

Sometimes a male penguin almost starves to death from lack of food while he incubates his egg. If he gets too hungry, he may abandon his egg on the ice and return to the sea to feed. Then the egg freezes and dies.

Sea Leopard

A leopard seal is a fast-moving, hungry hunter with a mouthful of sharp teeth. Leopard seals wait at the water's edge, ready to seize penguins as they leap into the sea. One spotted leopard seal was found with 160 pounds (73 kilograms) of penguin in its stomach, the weight of two or three adult emperor penguins!

Egg Thief

The giant petrel is a seabird that likes to feed on penguin eggs and chicks. This big bird swoops down and attacks prey with its strong, sharp bill. The petrel is powerful enough to kill even a penguin that is fully grown.

A Penguin's Day

5:00 AM

My little chick was asleep, snuggled up against me to keep warm. I looked forward to the Sun rising for the first time after the long, dark winter. Spring is here!

8:00 AM

My chick woke up hungry and begged for a meal. I regurgitated the food left in my stomach for her.

9:00 AM

It was cold, but not too windy. I was very hungry. I took my chick to a group of other chicks, where she could stay while I fished.

11:00 AM

I showed my chick how to slide on her belly. I think tobogganing is a great way to travel! She called out to tell her friends she was coming.

12:00 NOON

After sliding, my chick cuddled up with some other chicks. Two adults stayed to guard all the chicks. I slid off to a nearby hole in the ice to try to catch some fish.

3:00 PM

I managed to catch quite a few silverfish. The fish did not fill me up, but I was a little less hungry. As soon as my mate returns from her hunting trip, then I can go farther out to sea for a big fish.

5:00 PM

When I returned, I could tell the other penguins were upset. Some giant petrels had attacked and grabbed three chicks. My chick was one of the lucky ones.

6:00 PM

We tobogganed back to our usual place on the ice. I fed my chick a fishy meal.

8:00 PM

I preened my feathers and then put my head under my wing and settled down for a nap. My little chick cuddled up close and snoozed, too.

12:00 MIDNIGHT

I woke suddenly when I heard my mate calling from far away. I called back to guide her to us.

2:00 AM

I was glad that my mate came home safely. We bowed and called to each other. She fed our chick and cuddled together with us to stay warm. We slept soundly on the ice. I knew I had to leave soon to hunt for food in deeper water.

5:00 AM

It is time for me to go. I bowed and called good-bye, and then I swam away. I will be gone a few weeks.

Relatives

Penguins probably began to develop differently from flying birds about forty million years ago. Scientists think some ancient penguins were almost as tall as an adult human! Now there are about seventeen different kinds, or species, of penguins. They all have fairly large heads, short necks, and barrel-shaped dark and white bodies. Penguins range in size from the tiny fairy penguin, which stands 16 inches (40 centimeters) tall, to the emperor penguin, which is up to 4 feet (1.2 m) tall.

Crested Hoppers

Rockhopper penguins are colorful penguins. They have yellow and black feathery crests, bright orange-red bills, and striking red eyes. They are called "rockhoppers" because they jump to move from rock to rock. They even leap out of the sea onto the rocky coasts where they nest.

Fairy Penguin

The fairy penguin is the smallest of all the penguin species. These dark blue penguins live around the coasts of New Zealand and southern Australia. After fishing during the day, they go back to the beach and waddle to their burrows for the night.

Did You Know?

All adult penguins have dark-colored backs and light fronts. This color combination helps them hide from predators and prey when they swim in the sea. If a penguin is spotted from above, its dark back blends with the dark ocean, but if it is seen from below, its pale front blends with the lighter colors of the water at the surface.

Noisy Travelers

Adélie penguins build their nests on islands in the Antarctic. To travel to their breeding grounds, noisy groups of Adélie penguins waddle over 60 miles (100 km) across the ice. Their journey can take more than one week. Each step an Adélie penguin takes covers only about 4 inches (10 cm)!

Humans and Penguins

With their black-and-white coats and their unusual waddle, penguins are known and loved by people throughout the world. They are the heroes of many children's books and movies, and they star in wildlife shows. Penguins always seem to draw crowds in zoos. Penguins may be popular, but some species are fighting to survive as humans take over their habitat and **pollute** the environment.

Cold Vacation

In recent years, tourists have started to travel to Antarctica so they can watch penguins, seals, and whales in the wild. It's a chilly trip. Even in summer, temperatures hardly ever go above freezing. The breath of humans instantly turns into a mist of ice crystals. Lucky tourists, scientists, and photographers get a chance to see and hear all kinds of penguins at play.

Science Watch

No one lives in Antarctica all the time. The only humans there are scientists, soldiers, and tourists. Most of the time, scientists live in cozy underground bases. They study the animals, oceans, and weather. Many of the animals in Antarctica, such as the emperor penguin, are found nowhere else on Earth.

Did You Know?

- Early explorers killed penguins and salted the meat as food for their long sea journeys. Penguin blubber was used to make oil for lamps.
- Many people used to collect and eat penguin eggs. Collecting penguin eggs was stopped by law in 1969.
- Penguin feathers were once used for clothing, decoration, and mattress stuffing.

GLOSSARY

BREEDING
Related to reproducing or coming together for the purpose of producing young.

BURROWS
Tunnels or holes in the ground used as shelter by animals.

DOWN
Soft, fluffy feathers.

FLIGHTLESS
Unable to fly.

HABITATS
The natural settings in which plants and animals live.

ICE FLOE
A large, flat area of sea ice that floats freely in the ocean without connection to land.

INCUBATES
Keeps eggs warm so that they hatch into young animals.

MATES
Animal partners that come together to produce or raise young.

MOLT
To shed an outer covering of skin, hair, or feathers.

PACK ICE
Large pieces of floating sea ice that crowd together tightly in the ocean.

POLLUTE
To spoil the environment with human-made waste.

PREDATORS
Animals that hunt other animals for food.

PREENING
Cleaning and smoothing the feathers with the bill.

PREY
Animals that another animal hunts and kills for food.

REGURGITATED
Brought up swallowed and partly digested food. Penguins and other animals regurgitate food for their young to eat.

RUFFLES
Fluffs or roughs up something, such as feathers making them less smooth.

STREAMLINED
Having a smooth or flowing shape that moves easily through the air or water.

WADDLE
To walk with short steps while the front of the body swings from side to side.

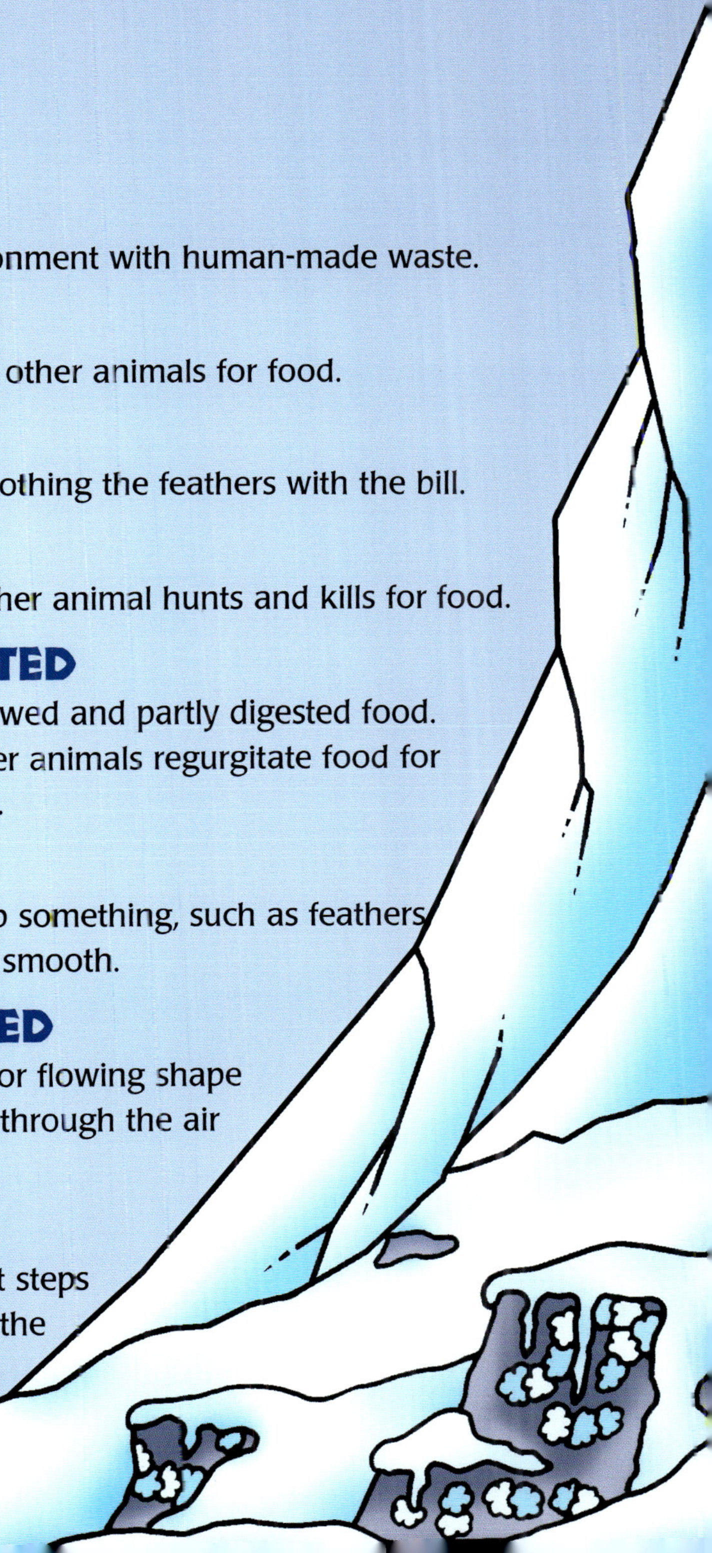

INDEX